Birthday

Holt, Rinehart and Winston ● **New York, Chicago, San Francisco**

John Steptoe
Birthday

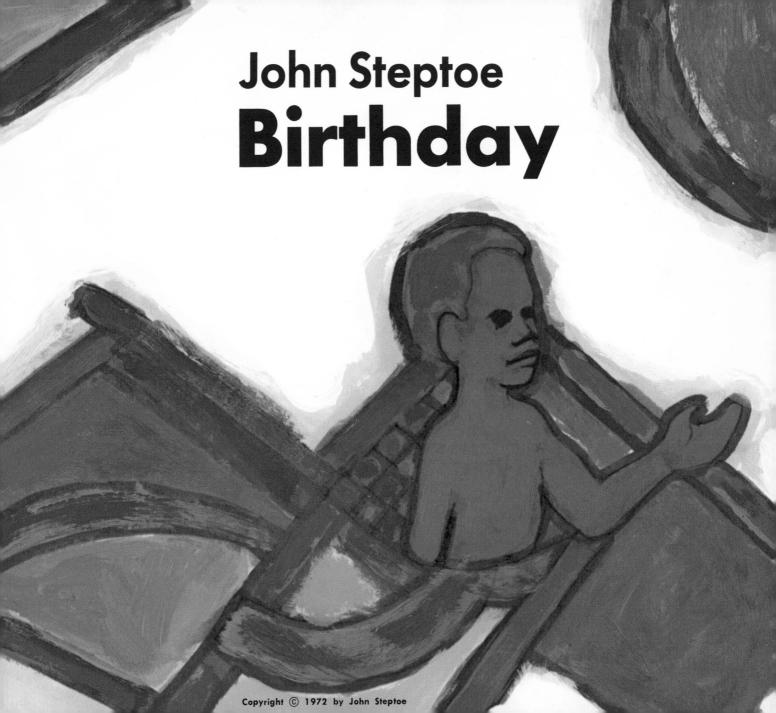

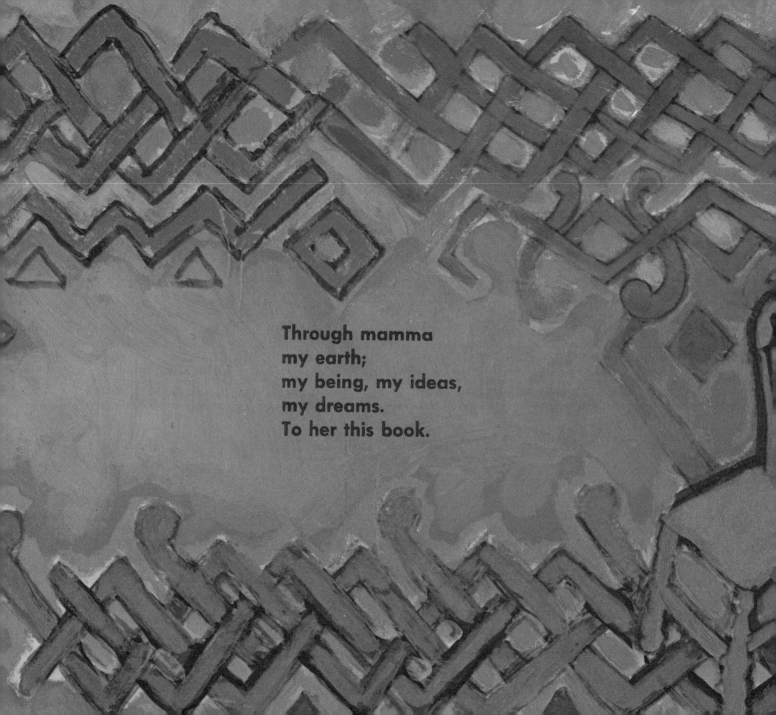

Through mamma
my earth;
my being, my ideas,
my dreams.
To her this book.

This morning I got up out of the bed real fast. Mamma only had to call me twice.

Today is gonna be the best day of my life, and I'm gonna have the most fun I ever had. Today is special and I'm special too because I was the firstborn in our new place, the first child of a whole new thing. My name is Javaka, and today is my eighth birthday.

We live right outside the brand-new town of Yoruba. My Daddy and his friends have farms around it. Yoruba is the name of a nation of people in Africa and my Daddy and his friends decided to name our place after it.

My Daddy always tells me about the time before we came here to live and the old America, where him and my Mamma used to live at. He says the people there didn't treat him like a man 'cause he was Black. That seemed stupid to me 'cause my Daddy is the strongest and smartest man alive.

Him and his friends couldn't live there no more 'cause if he didn't fight to leave, his life wouldn't be no good. When I grow up, I'm gonna be strong like my Daddy. I'm almost grown now, 'cause today I'm eight years old!

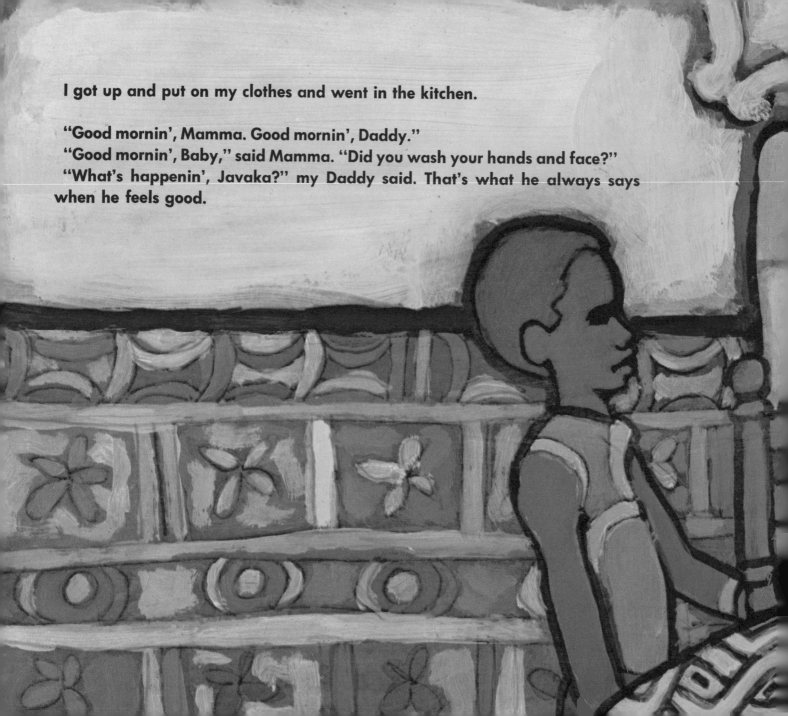

I got up and put on my clothes and went in the kitchen.

"Good mornin', Mamma. Good mornin', Daddy."
"Good mornin', Baby," said Mamma. "Did you wash your hands and face?"
"What's happenin', Javaka?" my Daddy said. That's what he always says when he feels good.

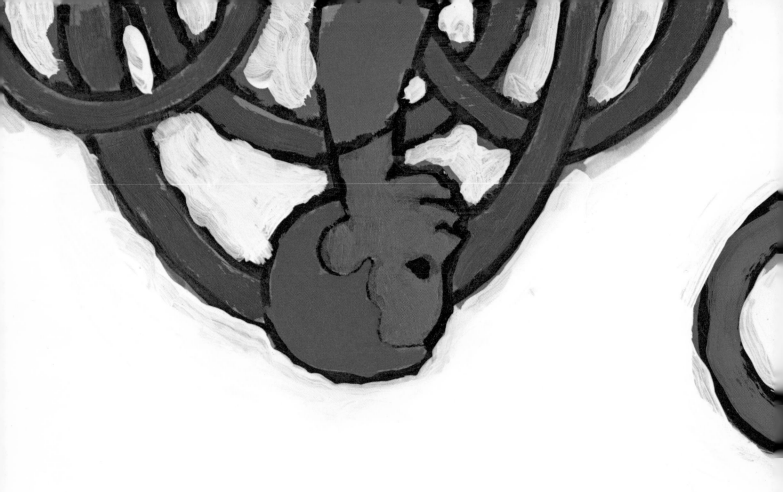

I felt good too. I sat down.

"Is everybody always happy, Daddy?" I asked.

"Some people are and some aren't. It's not easy to be happy. You have to work hard all the time for things you want. Just like we have to."

"But what do we need that we ain't got? I got you and Mamma and all my friends and a nice house. I like our house, Daddy. Will we ever have to leave?"

"Leave!? Why, Baby?" Mamma said.

"I don't know. You and Daddy said you all left from where you used to live."

"No, Javaka," my Daddy said, "This is our home, and we'll never have to leave."

"Good!" I said.

"Hurry up and get ready for school now," said Mamma.

On my way to school I was thinkin' it's nice where I live. I got a whole lot of friends here and we all go to school together.

Today when I got to class my teacher, Sister Naeima, said, "Now, sisters and brothers, who knows whose birthday it is today?"

Then everybody turned around. My best friend Baku stood up and said, "It's Brother Javaka's birthday."

"That's right!" said my teacher.
"Wasn't there something you were suppose' to tell the class, Javaka?"
So I stood up. My Mamma told me to tell everybody to come to my celebration after school. So I told them.

So right after school everybody followed me home. We took the shortcut through the marketplace and then across the square and down the road to my Daddy's and Mamma's and my farm.

When we got there, Mamma came out to welcome us. 'Most everybody's papas and mammas was there already. When there's a celebration it's time for everybody to party.

There were big clouds in the sky and it was a little bit hot. My Mamma made us some cold drinks.

Some of the mothers were helpin' Mamma cook. Our fathers had just come off the fields, all the animals were put away. I didn't have to do nothin' but party.

They had steel drums and bongos and horns that the men played. The music was boss, everybody was dancin' and singin' and the grown-ups was drinkin' rum and stuff.

My girl friend was there too, but she ain't really my girl friend, she just thinks she is. Her name is Tisha.

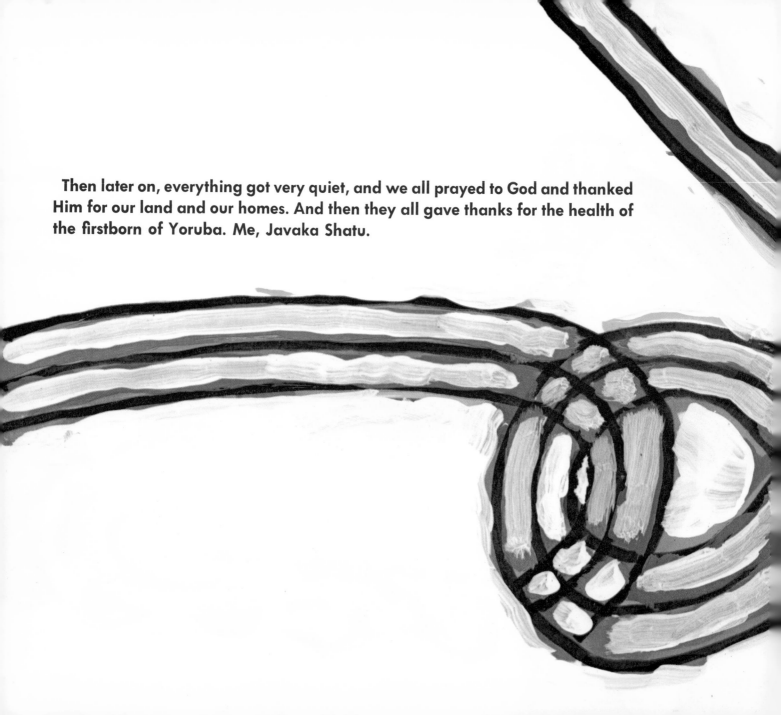

Then later on, everything got very quiet, and we all prayed to God and thanked Him for our land and our homes. And then they all gave thanks for the health of the firstborn of Yoruba. Me, Javaka Shatu.

Then we started the meal
and boy, did I grit back!

The food was boss, boy, my Mamma sure can cook! We had beef and chicken and fish and sweet potatoes and molasses cookies and peas and rice.

Then Mamma called to me, "Javaka, tell everybody your birthday wish."

I thought some, then I said something real corny but I meant it anyway.

"I hope that we all can live together like this forever."

That means "and peace be with you."

The party didn't end 'til three or four o'clock in the morning.
It was the best day I ever had!